Because I'm little, my owner gives me heart-shaped Mini Puppy Treats.

They're the MOST embarrassing things you've ever seen.

CHOOCHIE

Did you know that other dogs can laugh
and make you feel very small? Well, they can.

Outside the supermarket she said,

Then, when she came out,
she picked me up and she KISSED me,
so everyone could see. And she said,
"Off we go, CHOOCHIE POOH!"

Be honest. Do I look like I should be called *THAT*?

I gave her an angry look as if to tell her,

DON'T call me CHOOCHIE POOH!

But I don't think I'm good at angry looks because she said,

You're hungry, aren't you? LOOK, I've bought you some Mini Puppy Treats.

Then she put me
in her handbag!

What can you do?

We stopped in the park on the way home.
There were other dogs there.

AND CHIEF, WHO'S VERY BIG AND USED TO BE A POLICE DOG!

They were running about, barking, getting muddy and doing proper dog things.

Meanwhile I felt like a Mini-Puppy-Treat-eating-Choochie-Pooh in a handbag! And I thought they'd never ever want to play with me.

But I was wrong!
Because Chief looked at me
as if to say, "COME ON!"

So I did. And it was ...

BRILLIANT!

We played IT'S MY STICK!
(Where the main rule is you have
to growl as if you're really angry,
even though you're not.)

Then we played DOGS AND SAUSAGES!

(Which has complicated rules
that would take a long time to explain.)

And PUDDLE JUMPING!

(Which doesn't have any rules at all.)

I felt more over-excited than you can ever imagine.
It was like being a really proper dog!

What's more, Rusty, Bandit and Chief
all looked at me as if to say, "Come back
and play any time you want!"

THEN,
DISASTER STRUCK...

My owner called out,

I wanted to jump into a pit full of crocodiles.

I waited for my friends to laugh and make me feel very small. But actually ... Rusty's owner said,

Time to go home FIGGINS WIGGINS CUDDLE Pie!

And Bandit's owner said,

Come on, YOU LITTLE CUTIE PATOOTIE!

Then Chief's owner said,

"Let's go HUNKY PUNKY PUMPKIN BOTTOM!"

I looked at my new friends.

They looked at me.

We all looked at each other,
as if to say,

"What can you do?"

I play with them all the time now.

And I have to say that after all
the running and barking and
big dogs' games ...

even Mini Puppy Treats
taste quite good.

Don't Call Me CHOOCHIE POOH!

SEAN TAYLOR   KATE HINDLEY

TINY TINKER

PUPPY CONDITIONER

Eau de Pup

I might be little,
but I'm not one of those
silly dogs you get.